# ACKNOWLEDGEMENTS

First, thank you, God, you gave me everything I have. My life, my skills, the ability to do what I love, and its all just extra compared to knowing you; Every bit of art I make is for your fridge. Speaking of fridge art, thank you Mom and Tristan for supporting and believeing in me. I'm thankful for my career at Disney too, 10 years with Peter Pan taught me a lot about performing and storytelling. Tony Ley, I look up to you as a creator. Eric Sweetman, you were the first to inspire me to do watercolor. Bob Beckett, I woud not be an artist if it weren't for you. Thank you Lon Smart for being an awesome animator and even though you've had a Disney career I could only dream of, thank you for taking time to steal pizza with me and talk about art. Eddie Pittman thanks for being on my podcast and inspiring me with your awesome writing and art. Same to you Peter Raymundo, Tony Piedra, and the Sundy bros. Go buy 3rd Grade Mermaid, The Greatest Adventure, and Pancho Bandito respectively. They're awesome books. James Carbary, I'm so thankful to have you as a mentor and friend. I owe you every bit of business success I've had. Thank you to Orlando SCBWI, your workshops are better than college. Thank you to every teacher and media specialist who has welcomed me into your school, especially Becky Weso, Kristen Haynes, Sandra Young, Elanit Weizman, Elanna Fishbein, Kim Guilarte Gil, Olga Camarena, Victoria Laurrari, and Saili Hernandez. Thank you Ben Gamla, Pinecrest, Somerset, and all of Academica for welcoming me into your schools. Thank you to my 1100 followers on my facebook page; you never like anything I post but you hit that follow button! Thank you Instagram followers; you guys are way more engaged. Thank you to all 60 people who reviewed this book on Amazon. Thank you Stephen Mackey for being a huge encouragement to me. Thank you everyone who bought this book; you're the reason I get to do what I love.

Dinosaur Press Publishing

# THE POISONOUS WOODS

an adventure story
by TIMMY BAUER

In the Country of Dragons,
There's a field you should fear
Right next to some woods
You should NEVER go near.

The three boys were playing
Softball in the green

When out jumped a creature
They'd all never seen!

It ran for the ball
That flew to the trees.

"Oh no!!!"

"Come Back!"

Cried Jeff, Jim, and Steve.

But he ran in the woods,
Where he couldn't be seen.

"He's done for!" Jim said
With his head in his hand.
"Let's get him you goon!"
Came Stevie's command.

"But haven't you heard?" Said Jeffery in fear,
"Of the stories of people who've wandered in here?

Some have been eaten.
Some have been smooshed
Some have been ground up and turned into mush."

The dog stumbled out
While the three were debating
Right next to a picnic
Where Zoe was playing.
Steve missed that and figured he still needed saving.
They're not super bright, if you get what I'm saying.

There's no time to doddle, no time to discuss,
Let's get him before something finds him or us.

"Let's keep our eyes open! We can't even blink!"
Yelled Steve as Jim stepped into poop that was pink.

"Can we close our noses? Do you smell that stink?"

No we can't close our noses! Or we won't even smell,
We won't get the warning, we won't get the tell
That the horrible, stinkable "Big Bad Breath Beast"

Out searching for something to brush his gross teeth,
Will snatch you right up, use your head as his brush.

And just in case
That's            not awful enough,

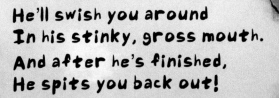

He'll swish you around
In his stinky, gross mouth.
And after he's finished,
He spits you back out!

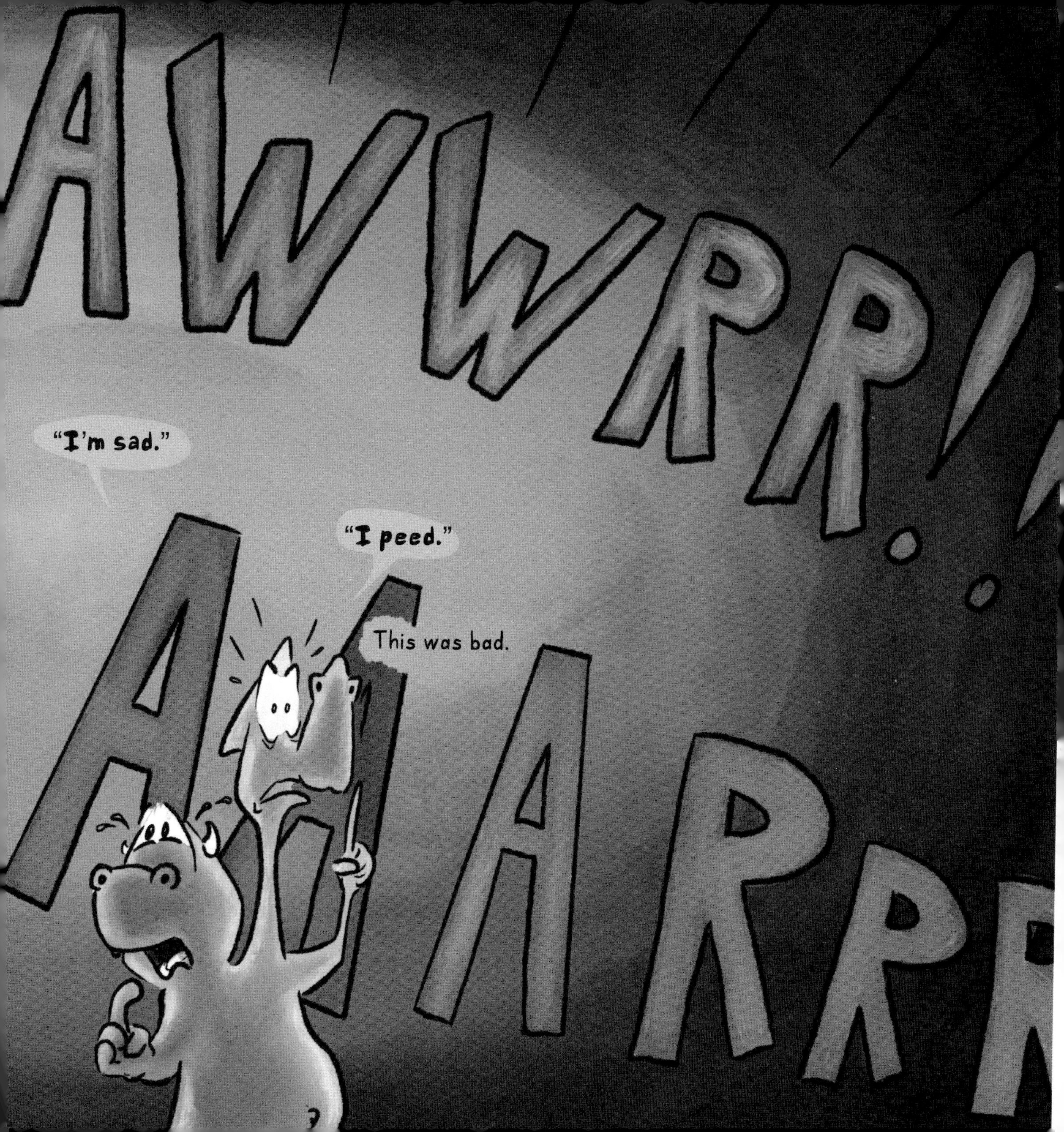
AWWRR!
"I'm sad."
"I peed."
This was bad.

Just as the three
Were all freaking out,
Steve noticed the ball.

"He must be around!"

It looked like the ball,
But it was an imposter.

This "ball" that they found
Was just a large nostril

Of a greyish-brown, scary,
Mean crocodile monster.

"Ouch! Your fingers!
They're crooked.
They're crinkled."

Another Steve saw
Was an egg that broke upen,
MILLIONS of spiders
Now were awoken!

Have you ever had spiders crawl up your NOSE?
Or go in your mouth? Or under your clothes?
Or tickle your armpits? Or live in your hair?
For Jeff, Jim, and Steve, they were EVERYWHERE.

So they abandoned the ball hunting plan
To ask for directions as much as they can.

They yelled to a rhino
That they tried to get near
It had 32 noses. And a large, bumpy rear.
But it didn't have ears
So he couldn't hear.

The Stinkus Flatulas.
He didn't help either.

Covered in bumps
Purple bruises and smells,
And surrounded by oak trees
as big as hotels.
**"We're now very lost,"**
They said to themselves.

Before they could think... before they could act
From every side, the roaring came back!

While it roared even louder than last time they heard it
Jim noticed a weird thing, and when he reached for it...

# AH!! AH

AH

AH

AH

AH

AH AH

AH

The three were yanked violently into the forest.

Back at the picnic,
Where Zoe was playing,
The little dog creature came up to her waving.

He dropped off the ball, and she held up a treat.
He semed to like that so she made him a seat.

"I'll call you Cookie.
You like them a lot.
Have you seen my brother?
He was right there I thought?
He was told not to leave me.
I guess he forgot.
Will you help me get him?"

He gave her a nod.

Zoe now started her trek through the trees.
With Cookie beside her, she followed the three.

Whose footprints were clearly laid out all around...

But froze in front of a weird thing she found.

A big, metal door
attached to a tree

Was it open?
They shrugged,
**"Let's try it and see."**

Zoe crept carefully down all the stairs.

There were beakers, and burners, and tubes everywhere.

Gauges

and gadgets.

Contraptions, tvs

Large microscopes at precise set degrees.

Reaching to grab the key from the rack,
She yelled,

"In a sec,
I'll be back for that snack!"

The end?

...no way!
To be continued...

Know the moment I finish my next book:
BillytheDragon.com/next

Watch my progress on Instagram
I post EVERYTHING.

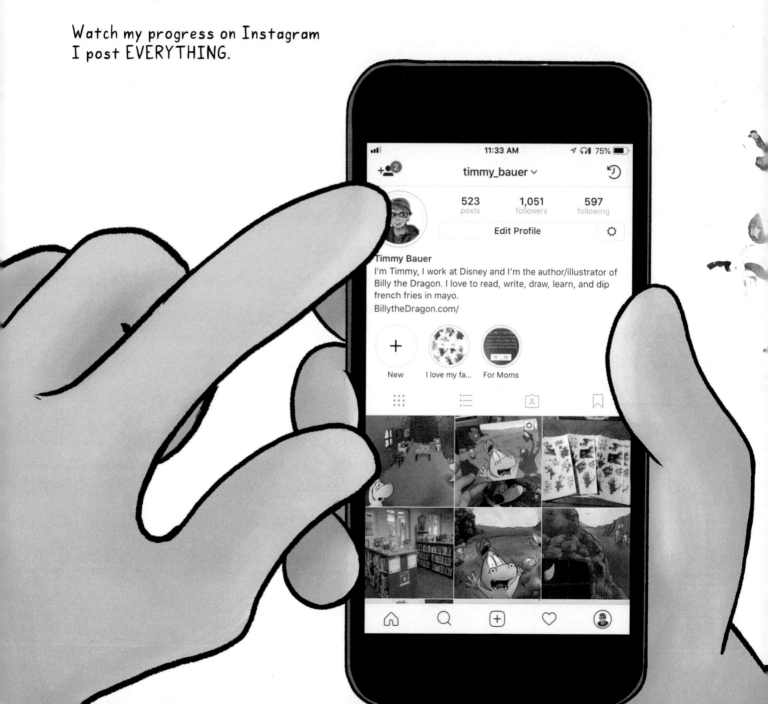

Made in the USA
Monee, IL,
16 January 2020